ASTONISHING ART

Susan Martineau

Illustrations by Martin Ursell

WINDMILL
BOOKS

New York

Published in 2012 by Windmill Books, LLC
303 Park Avenue South, Suite #1280, New York, NY 10010-3657

Adaptations to North American Edition © 2012 Windmill Books, LLC
© 2012 b small publishing ltd

Library of Congress Cataloging-in-Publication Data

Martineau, Susan.
Astonishing art / by Susan Martineau. — 1st ed.
p. cm. — (Awesome activities)
Includes index.
ISBN 978-1-61533-369-1 (library binding) — ISBN 978-1-61533-406-3 (pbk.) — ISBN 978-1-61533-469-8 (6-pack)
1. Handicraft—Juvenile literature. I. Title.
TT160.M374 2012
745.5—dc22
                                    2010052111

Manufactured in the United States of America

CPSIA Compliance Information: Batch #BS2011WM: For Further Information contact Windmill Books, New York, New York at 1-866-478-0556

Contents

You will need a bit of grown-up help in one or two places. These have been marked with this special symbol. ❗

Before You Begin

Start a junk collection! All kinds of old junk can be transformed into amazing artwork.

Boxes of all shapes and sizes

Old sponges

Make sure the junk is clean and dry before you store it. Boxes will take up less room if they are folded flat.

Old ribbons, shoelaces, hair elastics

Even onion skins and eggshells!

Don't forget to use old newspapers to cover work surfaces before you begin a project. To protect your clothes, you could wear an old shirt backward! Old detergent bottle caps make great containers for paints and glue. Empty tubes are good for storing pencils and pens.

Old clothes

Can tabs

Don't get too carried away collecting junk. Stop when you have a boxful and get cracking on some of the ideas in this book!

Aluminum foil

Cardboard, colored paper, and glitzy wrapping paper

Detergent bottle caps

Old photos and postcards

Corks

Are There Two of You?

Make a truly original **portrait** of yourself. You'll need some of your old clothes that don't fit any more. You could make portraits of your entire family or some friends, too.

What you will need:

- Large cardboard box
- Pencil
- Scissors
- A complete set of old clothes
- Plastic shopping bags (brown, yellow, black, or orange, depending on your hair color)

- Tape
- An old cork
- Markers
- Glue
- Brown or black wool or old hair elastics
- Red or pink wool or old hair elastics
- Old eraser

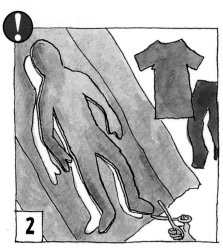

1 Open up the box and spread it out flat. Lie down on it. Ask a friend to trace your outline.

2 Cut out your cardboard self and dress it in your old clothes.

3 Cut strips of plastic bag. Cut hair as seen above. Tape it to the head.

Now create your face.
See the picture for ideas.

Cut slices of cork and color them to match your eyes.

Bits of brown or black wool or elastics work well for eyebrows.

Using scissors, shape a nose out of the eraser.

Use pink or red wool or hair elastics for the mouth.

Draw eyes and eyelashes.

☆☆☆☆☆ Snazzy Stamp ☆☆☆☆☆

Wrap masking tape around all but the tip of a vegetable peeler and use it to gouge out your own design in an eraser. Then dip the eraser in paint and use it as a stamp.

Wacky Weaving

How many plastic bags do you have lurking around your house? You could transform some of them into this snazzy woven bag. You will need to repeat steps 1 and 2 to make two pieces of weaving.

What you will need:
- Plastic bags in three different colors, cut into strips 1 inch (3 cm) wide
- Medium-sized cardboard box
- Scissors
- Tape

1 Tape strips of one color across the box. Weave strips of other colors in and out across the box.

Trim sides, leaving one fringed edge.

2 Put tape across all the edges of the woven area. Remove from box. Turn over and tape other side. Repeat steps 1 and 2 to make two pieces.

3 Tape two pieces of weaving together to form a bag. Cut the loose ends to make a fringe.

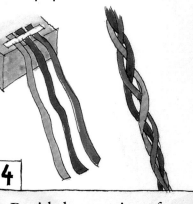

Tape plastic to a table.

4 Braid three strips of plastic. Tie knots at each end. Tape the ends to the bag to form a strap.

Onion Fish

Old onion skins make fantastic fish scales. Collect just the top layer of brown onion skin. You'll see that it's beautifully shiny inside. You could make a whole aquarium!

What you will need:

- Blue construction paper
- Pencil
- Onion skins
- Scissors
- Glue
- An old cork or some white cardboard
- Black marker

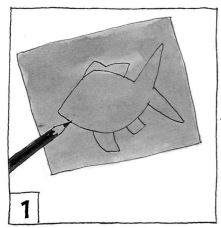

1

Lightly draw one or more fish outlines on the construction paper.

2 Leave fin and tail edges unglued for a 3-D effect.

Cut pieces of onion skin to make the fins, tail, and head. Glue them on, with the shiny side up.

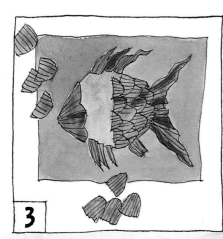

3

Cut out scales. Glue them on, with the shiny side up. Make them overlap. Start from the tail.

4

Cut a slice of cork or circle of cardboard for the eye. Draw a pupil in the middle with the marker. Glue it on.

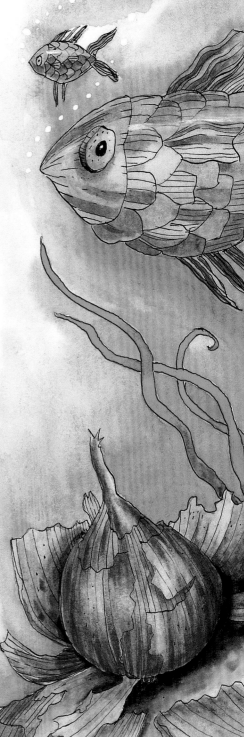

9

Big Box Croc

Leave this cardboard critter lying around to surprise your friends. He can be as big as you like. In fact, the bigger the better. You can use all those boxes you have been collecting for a rainy day.

What you will need:

- Eight or more rectangular or square boxes, of various sizes
- 5 egg cartons
- Cardboard from a cereal box
- Glue
- Tape

- Green, white, yellow, and black paint
- Paintbrushes
- String
- Scissors
- Metal skewer
- Pencil

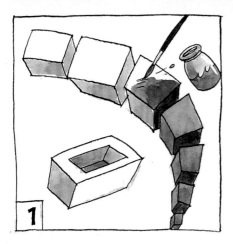

1

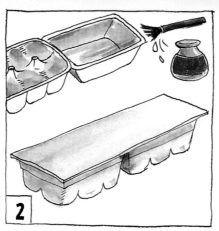

2

3

Start with the body. Lay all the boxes in a line, with the smallest ones at the tail. Remove the lids or cut a hole in each box, so you can put your hand inside. Paint the boxes green.

Make the head next. Glue two of the egg cartons shut. Lay them end to end. Cut a rectangle of cardboard to cover the top. Glue it in place.

Repeat step 2 with two other egg cartons. Cut two cups from the last egg carton. Glue them to the top of the head section.

THINK ABOUT IT!

Crocodiles have been around for nearly 200 million years, but they're now **endangered** because the swamps and rain forests they live in are being destroyed. Hunters also killed about 10 million crocodiles between 1870 and 1970 to make belts, shoes, bags, and wallets from their skins.

4 Glue teeth together.

Paint the teeth white and the rest of the head green. Once the paint is dry, glue the two head sections together. Paint two yellow eyes with black pupils.

5

With the skewer, make a small hole in each end of all the boxes. Thread a short length of string between each box and the next. Knot the ends inside.

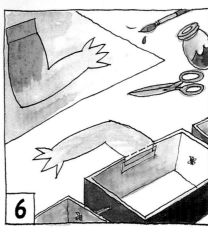

6

Draw two pairs of legs on the cardboard. Paint them green, let them dry, and then cut them out. Fold a small flap at the end of each limb. Tape firmly inside the body boxes.

Masterful Masks

Elephant Ears

This very simple idea uses old egg cartons and cardboard.

What you will need:
- 2 egg carton lids
- Gray paint and a paintbrush
- Scissors
- Tape
- Thin cardboard from a cereal box
- Pencil
- Elastic

1

First paint the lids gray. If your egg carton is already gray, you can skip this step.

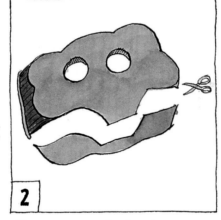

2

Cut two eyeholes in one lid. Cut away one edge, as shown, to make the head shape and start the trunk.

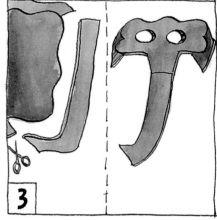

3

Cut a strip from one side and corner of the other lid to make a trunk. Tape it to the head.

4 Paint the ears gray if necessary.

Draw two ear shapes on the cardboard. Cut them out and tape them to the sides of the head, as seen above.

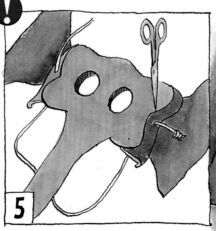

5

Make a hole in each side of the head with the point of the scissors. Thread the elastic through and tie knots as shown.

Foxy Features

Make a fox face using cardboard and old sponges. You could also make other animals, such as rabbits, badgers, and bears, using the same basic idea.

What you will need:

- Cardboard from a cereal box
- Pencil
- Scissors
- Crayons
- Toilet paper tube
- A yellow, orange, or white sponge
- Glue
- Elastic

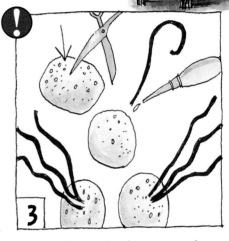

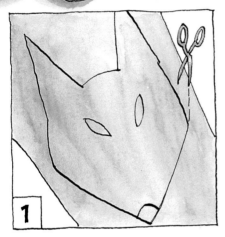

1 Draw a fox face on the cardboard. Cut it out. Cut two holes for eyes as shown. Color it orange with a black nose.

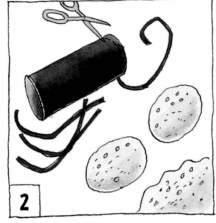

2 Color the toilet paper tube black. Cut six very thin strands for whiskers. Cut two small cheeks from sponge.

3 Make three holes in each sponge. Dip the end of each whisker in glue. Stick three whiskers into each cheek.

4 Glue the cheeks to the face. Make holes for the elastic. Thread it through and tie knots to finish.

Crazy Cuttings!

This is a perfect way to use up old, unwanted family photos once the best ones are in the album. Recycle those old postcards and magazines that are gathering dust, too.

WARNING!
Please make sure the photos are not prized family portraits before you start cutting them up!

What you will need:
- Old family photos, especially ones with you in them
- Old magazines
- Old postcards
- Scissors
- Glue

1 Cut out the heads from the photos. Remove as much of the background as possible.

2 Sift through postcards for scenes with people in them. Sort through the magazines to find your favorite stars.

3 Now start placing the photo heads on top of the heads in the postcards and magazine pictures. See which ones look best!

THINK ABOUT IT!

Most paper collected for recycling is made into yet more paper. It could end up as anything from elegant stationery to toilet paper and cardboard boxes. However, it could also end up as fuel, building materials, cars, shoes, or kitty litter!

You can stick your sneaky pictures on your wall or send them to a friend. Autograph your "fan" shots. Now you're a celebrity!

4

Glue the heads in place. Cut out the magazine pictures.

You're Framed!

You could make a simple frame from old pieces of cardboard.

Backing cardboard

Front of the frame

Paint the pieces of cardboard, or cover them with old wrapping paper.
Glue them together on three sides only. Leave one side open to slide in your creation.

Jurassock Park

Create your own dinosaurs out of old socks. The following are just some ideas to get you started. You can make up your own **prehistoric** pets, too!

What you will need:

- Clean old socks
- Markers
- Toilet paper tube
- Scissors
- Used but clean sponges and scouring pads
- Needle and thread
- Old red or pink ribbon

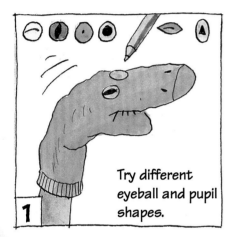

1

Try different eyeball and pupil shapes.

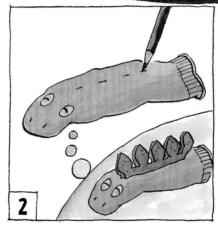

2

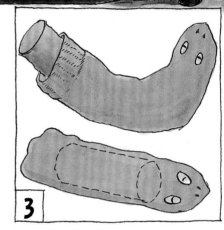

3

Put the sock on your hand, with your thumb in the heel. Draw eyes and nostrils with the markers.

Lightly mark where you would like to put spines, horns, and other features.

Take off the sock and push the toilet paper tube inside it. This should stop you from sewing right through the sock.

Top Triceratops

Cut a frill out of a large, stiff, green scouring pad. Cut three horns from the same pad. Sew into place.

Stegosockus

Cut two rows of bony plates out of a stiff scouring pad. Sew it into place.

Mighty Meat-Eater

Cut some rows of teeth out of a sponge. Stitch them inside the mouth. Cut a tongue out of ribbon. Sew it into place.

☆☆☆☆☆ **Puppet Pets** ☆☆☆☆☆

Socks can be made into all kinds of weird and amazing puppet creatures. Just look at your junk collection and see what else you can use. Old wool, string, or strips of plastic bag work as fur or a mane. Beads and buttons make great eyes.

On Guard!

Save up as much old aluminum foil as you can to make your own medieval armor. Design your own **emblem** for the shield using any old ribbons, colored paper, or shiny wrapping paper that you can find.

Shiny Shield

Tape doesn't show up on tinfoil, so it doesn't matter how many pieces you have to use to cover the shield.

What you will need:
- Large piece of cardboard
- A pencil and scissors
- Old, clean aluminum foil
- Tape
- Things to use for decoration

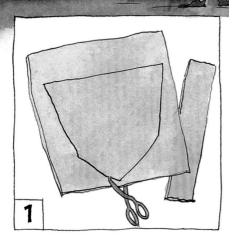

1

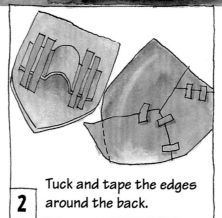

Tuck and tape the edges around the back.

2

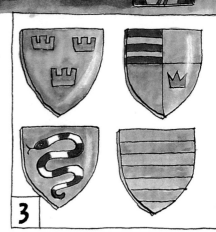

3

Draw the outline of your shield on the cardboard. Cut it out. Cut out a wide strip of cardboard, too.

Tape the wide strip to the back of the shield as shown. Cover the front of the shield with pieces of foil.

Add your own personal emblem to finish.

Short Sword

If you find a large enough piece of cardboard, you can make this a long jousting sword instead!

1 Draw the shape of the sword blade on the cardboard. Cut it out.

What you will need:

- Thick cardboard
- Pencil
- Scissors
- Disposable aluminum baking dish
- Old, clean aluminum foil
- Tape

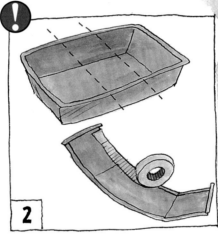

2 Cut a wide strip from the foil dish. Fold it over and put tape along the cut edges.

3 Cover the blade with tinfoil. Cut a slit in the middle of the foil strip. Slide the blade through the slit. Use tape to hold it in place.

THINK ABOUT IT!

The garbage left behind in the ancient trash pits of castles can give us a clear picture of what life might have been like then. For example, animal bones tell us what people ate.

Eggy Mosaics

You can make **mosaics** from all kinds of junk. Just look at your collection of stuff and try out different materials. Simple patterns, flags, and heraldic emblems all make great designs.

Terra Cotta Eggshells

Collect empty eggshells from cooking or from hard-boiled eggs. Wash them out and let them dry. Six half shells will be enough to make a picture about 6 inches (16 cm) long and 5 inches (14 cm) wide.

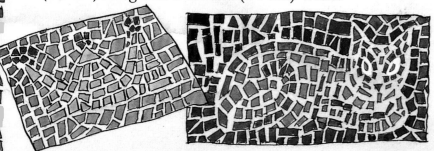

What you will need:
- Eggshells
- Paints in different colors
- Paintbrushes
- Paper
- Pencil
- Glue

You don't need to paint right to the edge of the shells.

1

Paint some of the eggshells different colors. Let them dry. Leave some shells unpainted, too.

Draw a rough draft first using colored pencils.

2

Draw your design on the paper lightly in pencil. Decide where you want each color to go.

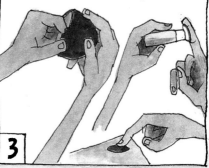

Bend the edges of the shells with your nails to shape them.

3

Break off bits of shell and apply glue. Press them into place. The eggshell will crack, but the "skin" inside will hold it together.

☆☆☆☆☆ The Finishing Touch ☆☆☆☆☆

Finish your mosaic by varnishing it. Mix 1 teaspoon of liquid glue with 3 teaspoons of water. Brush the mixture lightly across the mosaic. It will become clear when it dries.

Magazine Mosaic

Sort through old magazines and catalogs and look for solid blocks of color. You will need about four different colors to work with. Slightly different shades of the same color are fine. Clothing catalogs are really good for solid patches of one color.

What you will need:
- Old magazines or catalogs
- Scissors and glue
- Plain paper and pencil
- Envelopes or plastic pots to keep the colored squares separate

Do the background last.

1 Cut out solid areas of your chosen colors. Cut them into small squares.

2 Draw your design in pencil first.

3 Add glue a small area of the outline at a time. Then fill it in with squares. If whole squares will not fit, cut them to fill the space.

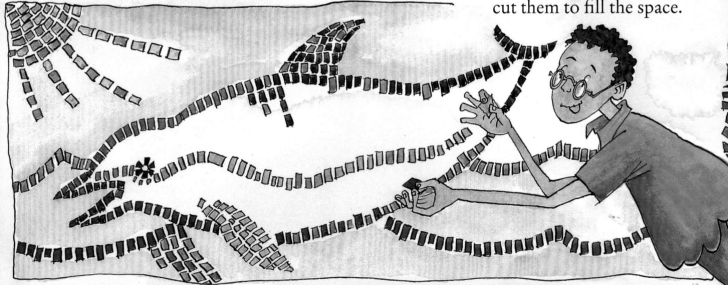

THINK ABOUT IT!

Roman public baths were often decorated with mosaics. Dolphin designs were very popular. At the Roman baths in Timgad, in North Africa, carved dolphin armrests were even placed between each seat!

Fit for a Pharaoh

This Egyptian-style collar is guaranteed to impress your friends.

Jewelled Collar

Ask your friends to help you collect loads of can tabs. You will need as many different colors as possible for the jewels!

What you will need:
- An old T-shirt
- Colored pencils and paper
- Pinking shears
- Can tabs
- Needle and thread

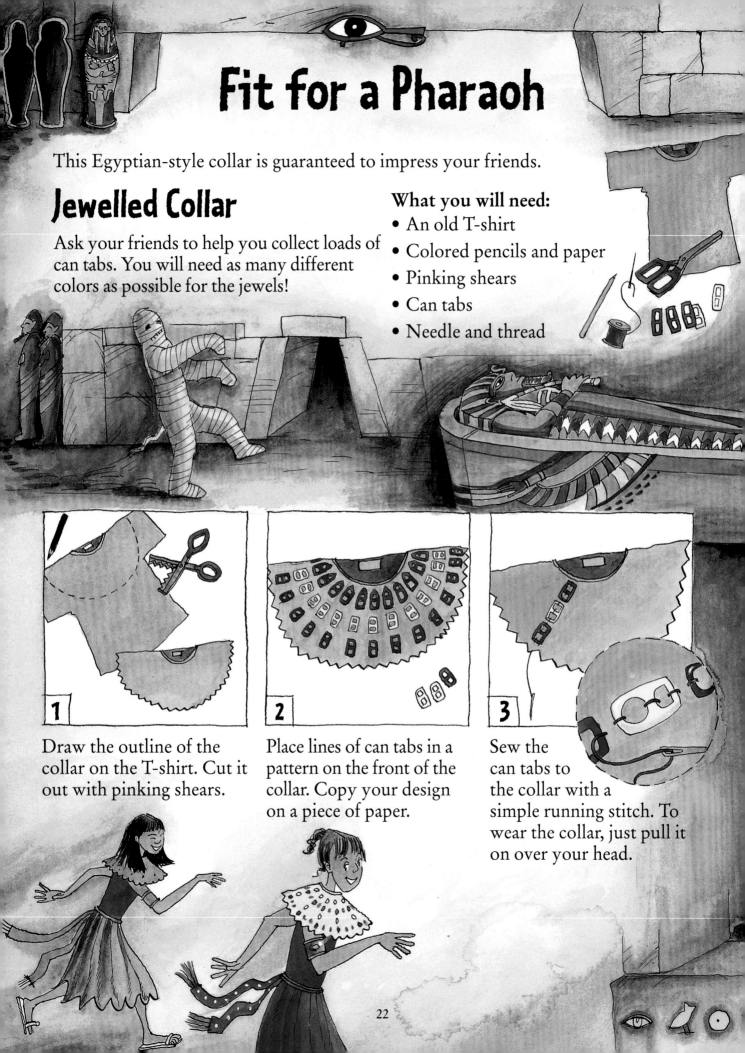

1 Draw the outline of the collar on the T-shirt. Cut it out with pinking shears.

2 Place lines of can tabs in a pattern on the front of the collar. Copy your design on a piece of paper.

3 Sew the can tabs to the collar with a simple running stitch. To wear the collar, just pull it on over your head.

Amulet Armlet

Wear this embossed armlet on your upper arm in true Ancient Egyptian style. The eye design is the Eye of Horus. It is the protective sign of the sky god! You could also invent designs of your own.

What you will need:
- 1 toilet paper tube
- Scissors
- Thick string or an old shoelace
- Glue
- Silver or gold foil

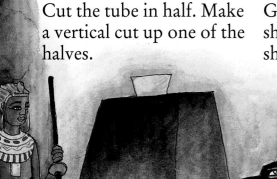

1 Cut the tube in half. Make a vertical cut up one of the halves.

2 Glue on pieces of string or shoelace in an eye design as shown. Let it dry.

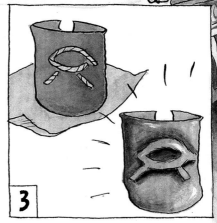

3 Carefully cover the tube with a piece of foil. Gently press around the eye design.

THINK ABOUT IT!

Unfortunately, Ancient Egyptian **mummies** have not always been treated with respect. Ground-up mummy used to be made into medicines during the sixteenth and seventeenth centuries.

Read More

D'Cruz, Anna-Marie. *Make Your Own Puppets*. New York: PowerKids Press, 2009.

Johnson, Karen. *Super Duper Art & Craft Activity Book: Over 75 Indoor and Outdoor Projects for Kids*. San Francisco: Chronicle Books, 2005.

Martin, Laura C. *Recycled Crafts Box*. North Adams, Massachusetts: Storey Books, 2004.

Glossary

emblem (EM-blum) A picture that stands for a person or group.

endangered (in-DAYN-jerd) In danger of no longer living.

mosaics (moh-ZAY-iks) Pictures made by fitting together small pieces of stone, glass, or tile and pasting them in place.

mummies (MUH-meez) Bodies prepared for burial in a way that makes them last a long time.

portrait (POR-tret) A picture, often a painting, of a person.

prehistoric (pree-his-TOR-ik) Having to do with the time before written history.

Index

Web Sites

For Web resources related to the subject of this book, go to: www.windmillbooks.com/weblinks and select this book's title.